I0825645

THE YOUNG DETECTIVES

The Hijacking of the Boeing 707

Jerry Gomez Shor Jr.

The Young Detectives:
The Hijacking of the Boeing 707

All Rights Reserved
© 2018, Jerry Gomez Shor Jr.
© 2018, Illustrations:
Jerry Gomez Shor Jr. & Camilo Quevedo
© 2018, Cover:
Jerry Gomez Shor Jr. & Camilo Quevedo

Pukiyari Editores

The total or partial reproduction of this book is prohibited. This book cannot be totally or partially reproduced, transmitted, copied or stored using any means or ways including graphic, electronics or mechanic without the consent and written authorization of the author, except in the case of small quotes used in articles and written comments about the book.

ISBN-10: 1-63065-106-0
ISBN-13: 978-1-63065-106-0

PUKIYARI PUBLISHERS
www.pukiyari.com

Dedication

To my dear readers

The English have the famous detective Sherlock Holmes of Sir Arthur Conan Doyle. The French have the famous Villain Arsenio Lupine and his rival Herlock Sholmes of Maurice LeBlanc. United States has Auguste Dupin created by Edgard Allan Poe. And Perú will have Ayesha and Schariar, the young detectives, who with the typical and unique Latin craftiness will solve police cases.

I dedicate this second chapter to every lover of true justice and to my mother, who was partly the architect of the creation of these characters and who taught me certain writing tricks.

Prologue

I woke up early that Monday, it was a Monday like any other. I was starting another week with the same routine where I would go every day to the same boring job I've been doing for many years. It was the monotony of being a supermarket cashier, smiling at all the customers and listening to their never-ending complaints. That day, after getting a good cold-water shower to wake up and then going to the kitchen to prepare my morning coffee and my mushroom omelette sandwich, I sat at the table to eat. I was taking the first bite when I saw a yellow envelope half-opened, some printed papers were showing. It was a rather thick envelope slid halfway through the living room window.

I stared at it with extreme curiosity, and started to ponder if I left it there, or if someone else did so.

What could this be...? I thought for a moment... until I remembered that nameless friend, an old man, that I met on one of those bohemian nights in a bar near the beach, and who, between beers, told me a story of some anonymous detectives who twarted many criminal acts without the press or media ever finding out. Through a common friend, he got the scoop on the stories and wrote them down long time ago.

I was taking the first bite when I saw a yellow envelope half opened, some written papers were showing. It was a rather thick envelope slid halfway through the living room window.

As you, my dear readers, may remember, I got the first manuscript some time ago. It was "The Case of the Thirteen Gold Coins." And after that, I never heard back from him.

This older gentleman had promised me that he would send me periodically more chapters about the young detectives. And because I had connections in the media, this would make it easy to publish the exclusive, so everyone could find out about what had happened.

I left my breakfast half eaten and after standing up I walked to the window and took that yellowish envelope. As I opened it, I went back to the table and started to pull the papers out of it. Looking at them, I had the feeling they had been printed long time ago. On top of all those papers was a note that seemed written recently. It was a letter and I recognized his handwriting. It said:

Dear friend,

Since a promise is a debt, I'll be trusting you with the second part of this extraordinary story that mysteriously came to me from one of the acquaintances of the young detectives, a long time ago. As you know, you must keep my name and theirs undisclosed, since events and state secrets that should not be disclosed are revealed in these stories.

I bid you farewell with a strong hug.

Your friend, an anonymous old man

And that's how the letter ended, leaving me surprised and curious, as I usually feel when something new takes me out of my daily routine.

It has been more than three months since the day this letter arrived. And today I received in my house the first shipment of boxes full of books with this second story to distribute; that you, my dear readers, will enjoy.

Thank you,

Your author.

THE HIJACKING OF THE BOEING 707

Part I
The Escape

It was a dark and grim night, too quiet for a place like the "Castro Castro" prison in the district of Canto Grande in Lima. The guards who worked that night, about three at the front door and two in the control towers located in both corners to the side of the entrance, began to feel restless, they did not know what it was, but something bad seemed to be coming their way.

Meanwhile, on the left side of the penitentiary building and one hundred meters away, two suspicious people wearing ski masks were waiting for the right moment to act.

It was about two in the morning when one of them said to his buddy:

"It's time. Can you see the door?"

"Yes," his partner answered. "There's five guards. Two of them went inside for the change of guards, so we only have three minutes to get going. You know what to do, right?"

"Of course, buddy. Don't worry."

Inside the penitentiary, the guards marched from one side to the other, turning in the corner and following their route some forty more steps before turning on their heels and returning.

It was at that precise moment, before turning, that one of the guards was taken down by one of the hooded men, who quickly undressed him and, after putting on his uniform, hid his body in the bushes that grew near the wall.

Without pausing, the hooded man took the place of the guard.

Once his partner did the same, they started to walk toward the door as if they were the real guards.

It took them just a few steps to get near the third guard. Again, they took him down, they gagged him and hid him in the bushes with the others.

They continued with their rounds until it was time to change guards. At that point they only had two or three minutes left before it was done.

Sure enough, three minutes later another three guards came to replace them, but when they noticed the third guard was missing they asked what had happened. To which the two replied he went out for cigarettes. The new guards were quite surprised by that strange response, since it was forbidden to leave the post, but they had no choice but to accept it and take the turn of the two.

They exchange a few words about how quiet it had been, and the two groups of guards went their separate ways.

After entering the prison, the two thugs disguised as guards took a corridor that led them to the basement. They approached the office of reports, or at least that was what the sign read, although it was a small dirty desk with a few shelves on its side with papers that apparently seemed useless. They tried to greet the custodian, but he was deeply asleep and completely alone, so it was easy for them to gag and hide him. Then they looked through the papers for the names of their colleagues who were imprisoned.

After a few seconds one of them exclaimed:

“Look, boss. I found him! They’re on Block 6, "crimes against property". Juan and Edward are in cell 8, Carlos and Gregory in cell 9 and Fabian is in 10.”

“Perfect,” his partner replied, “Now we just need to locate that block inside this maze.”

The moment he finished stating this, he realized that right in front of him was a detailed map of that penitentiary. Looking through it, they realized they should go to the second basement, which was directly underneath Block 6. They were ready to start moving, but before they left they took the custodian's uniform, so they could give it to one of their partners, once they rescued them.

They started walking through the cold and damp passageway, until they came across two guards who guarded an iron fence that blocked the way to the stairs that went down to the second basement. After greeting them military style, they were told that they needed a special permit to go beyond that point and that if they did not have that authorization, they could not enter because it was a restricted area. After receiving that response, the boss made as if he were to take a piece of paper out of his pocket and winking at his partner instead he gave a sharp blow to one of the guards, leaving him unconscious instantly and, before the other could react, the boss's mate hit his neck, leaving him unconscious. They tied and hid them, taking also their uniforms and weapons.

When they opened the doorway, they saw two guards coming their way.

As you can imagine, dear readers, the thugs got extremely nervous. The boss said to his buddy that if the guards already had realized they did not belong there, they would have no choice but to take good care of them (meaning they would have to disable the guards for a long time, or even kill them).

But their worries were too much, the guards only came for the change of shift; so, they exchanged greetings informing that everything was fine and they continued on their way.

They had already walked a large stretch of the passageway and were approaching Block 4, when they again encountered more guards; this time there were four.

"What should we do, boss?" said his assistant.

"Don't worry," he answered while he kept walking. "Keep moving. I'll think of something. But when I do, you must follow my lead."

"Of course, boss."

Once they approached and greeted each other military style, the boss, who wore a lieutenant uniform, ordered them to give way as they came to pick up a prisoner by court order. The guards, confused, asked them about the proper authorization. The boss's partner was at the peak of nervousness and believed that his boss had been wrong this time. When he suddenly noticed that the boss pulled a piece of paper out of his pocket and handed it to one of the guards. When the guard read it, he was confused.

"This prisoner was processed two days ago," he said.

The boss raised his voice and screaming with natural indignation said:

"Are you going to deny my authority to these guards when I come with the proper authorization of the judiciary to enter the crime against property block?"

"Of course not, lieutenant," answered the guard, who actualy was a sergeant, who then let them through with a salute.

After they got further away from the guards, one of the thugs said to the other:

"How come you had that official authorization from the judiciary?"

"When you get to have my level of experience and contacts, you'll be able to get whatever you want in any country," the boss answered.

They were getting closer and closer to Block 6, the only obstacle they needed to figure out was how to disarm two more guards who guarded the entrance gate to the building. So far everything had gone well, but the assistant's concern was how to get out of there after everything, he did not want to go back the same way they entered, but he had some confidence that being with his boss they would achieve their objective one way or another. He was immersed in this thought when they ran into the guards and, almost without realizing it, his boss disarmed the two and, after tying them, they continued on the road until finally they reached cell 8. These were small, dirty and smelly rooms, which would hardly have enough space for two inmates in each one; however, there would be three, four and even five prisoners in each chamber piled up as if they were animals. They were feeling sad for the inmates until they saw Juan and Edward and they opened the gate slowly so that they left, leaving it closed as if nothing had happened. Then they continued to free Carlos, Gregory and Fabian.

After putting on the uniforms of the guards, they continued walking, but not the way they had entered. Instead, they kept going down the passage, between the cells. Some were confused, but they trusted their boss, they followed without question. They entered a dark corridor and headed downhill; they could hardly see, but there were no guards, from time to time they'd heard the moaning of inmates asking for food, they assumed it came from those with lifetime sentences. They wanted to free them but knew they would run the risk of being caught again.

Their walk lasted about ten to fifteen minutes, which seemed endless until they hit a wall. From there on, the only way to reach the outside world was a ladder attached to the wall; and after leaving that totally vertical tunnel they would find themselves in a small platform to the side of the patio where the prisoners were led out at noon to breathe some fresh air.

It was about three o'clock in the morning and the place was silent, no guard could have imagined that by morning five prisoners would have escaped. Crawling on hands and knees, and after cutting some wires, they passed below an iron fence that surrounded the patio. From there they only had to go some thirty or forty meters towards the wall of about four meters high; after which they would be free.

There were only two guards in that area and in between each time they came together to the same place and crossed each other the thugs had exactly three minutes to pass before they turned on their heels and went through the area again. You can imagine, dear readers, how tense everyone was, although the worst was already behind them, they still had a small stretch to cover; and if one failed, all would fail.

They stepped up one by one until the seven reached the other end. Once there, ready and rested, Smith ordered them to look for a rope thrown from the outside by Betty. It was incredible, every detail had been planned. After a while, Edward found it, about eight meters away from where they were. But before starting to climb, Smith reminded them that they had exactly three minutes to get to the rope, climb and jump out before the guards turned around. Once on the other side of the wall, two blocks to the left, they would find the truck with Betty at the wheel.

"We will meet there. But, if for some reason the last ones to leave take more than twenty minutes, we will have to leave them behind and take off. Even if it is me. We'll see how we'll get out of this one!"

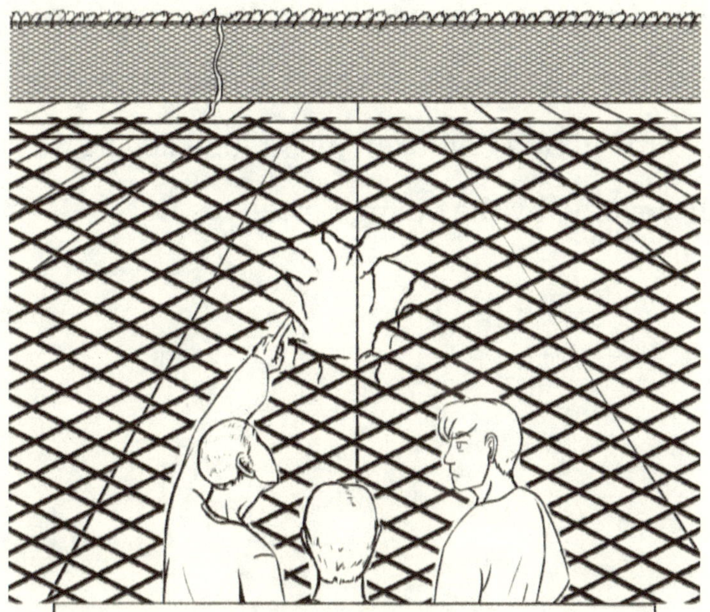

But before starting to climb, Smith reminded them that they had exactly three minutes to get to the rope, climb and jump out. Once on the other side of the wall, two blocks to the left, they would find the truck and Betty.

Happily everything went perfect, the seven met in the van and left for their new secret shelter located somewhere in Vipol, in the district of San Martín de Porras in Lima; because the old one, as you will remember, was destroyed by a bomb left by Smith when he was discovered by the young detectives.

Part II
An Intervention

That afternoon the two friends were at an exhibit of ancient relics that included written tablets and papyri, as well as woven and fine metals artifacts. What caught Schariar's immediate attention were the writings and numerology of the ancient humans. It was so compelling, he tried to memorize the whole display before him. Ayesha did the same because she was also impressed by the figures, lines and points that, united in different ways, could easily express a message, what she could not understand was why Schariar drew each of them without losing any detail. When she could no longer stay just wondering what was going on, she asked him why he was doing that.

"I have an excellent idea, Ayesha, when we get home I'll explain everything to you," he replied.

"Okay, Schariar, as you wish," she answered and trying to joke with him, she added, "So, I have another great idea, my friend. Help me take this skeleton of brontosaurus, to scare away evil spirits."

"Come on Ayesha don't make laugh… it'll break my concentration."

Ayesha left him alone for a moment and began to explore the entire gallery. There were complete skeletons of almost all the dinosaurs that existed on earth and fish of different shapes and sizes. As she walked and listened to what the guide said about each show in the exhibition, her mind at times flew thinking of Schariar. She did not know what it was, but Ayesha had a feeling that she'd never had felt towards someone, although she couldn't figure out if it was respect, affection or love. She had never been in a relationship with a guy, so she could not know for sure how it was supposed to feel; but Ayesha knew that she could not go on being without him for many days. Schariar, on the other hand, seemed to only see her as a friend. To her, it was his personality, his way of speaking and behaving that made him different from others, she had never heard him complain about any situation, he firmly believed that everything can be done and that nothing is impossible. Schariar gave her confidence and encouraged her to fight for what she wanted.

While deep in her thoughts, Ayesha heard Schariar telling her it was time to leave.

"But why? There's so much you have to see," she said to him.

But it was obvious that he had many ideas in mind and did not want to waste time. Schariar wanted to get home and write everything down.

They left Museo de la Nación, on Javier Prado Avenue, in San Borja, Lima, and they drove back to the apartment in Schariar's car.

While they were still in traffic, Ayesha fell asleep resting her head on Schariar's shoulder and he hugged her almost without thinking. It was the first time that the girl felt the heartbeat of someone other than her father. She wanted to kiss him, but she restrained herself to avoid any kind of misinterpretation since Schariar was more conservative than her.

When they got to the apartment building, they went upstairs almost without talking, and as soon as Ayesha saw her bed she only managed to lie down and sleep for a while.

The nap took longer than she thought. Three hours later Ayesha woke up when Schariar started to call out to her. He was finally ready to explain his idea.

"Remember the hieroglyphics we saw at the museum?"

"Of course. The only thing you did while we were there was to draw them."

"Yes. That took me to create a new code language that only the two of us will use when we need to communicate in case of emergency or if we don't want others to know what we are saying," he replied with glee.

"Okay, Schariar, you know that what you're saying is ridiculous, right? This is stuff you only see in the movies," Ayesha replied without knowing that later on it would be her who would use that code language, as you, my dear readers, will soon learn.

"Let's do this in steps: first, the alphabet. It's not the same we saw in the museum. I've modified it, and you can see it now," Schariar said as he showed her his invention.

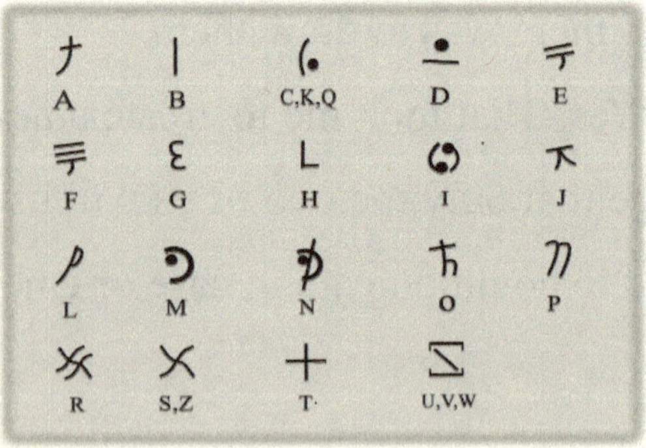

"And now the numbers. As you can see, Ayesha, they are very similar to the ones the Mayas used."

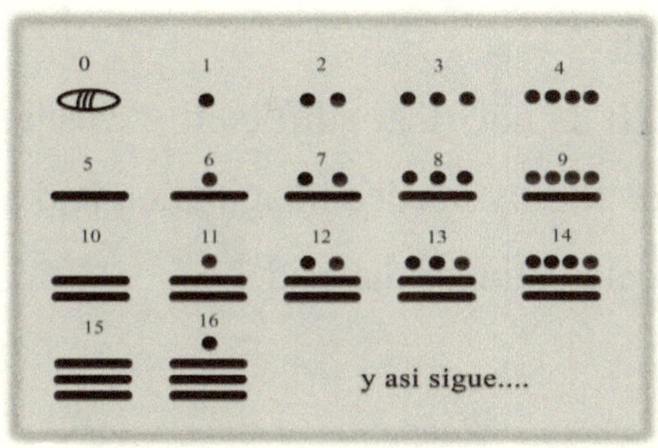

"As you can see, Ayesha, the numbers seem difficult, but they are not. The point is a sign that represents a digit and can be combined with others; for example, with the line, which is another four-digit sign. You only have to join and / or combine these signs to write a quantity. And you can even perform mathematical operations as easily as with conventional numbers known universally," Schariar explained.

"You are a genius," she exclaimed. "I can't believe you created our own code language."

"It's not that difficult, Ayesha," he replied, "I only needed imagination and a little bit of calculations," he said.

Part III
The Search

The next day the news about the disappearance of five prisoners from the safest prison in the country were on television, radio and the front page of newspapers. The authorities did not know how to explain at what moment two people were able to enter and so easily evade the strong surveillance of the prison; the alarm and cameras scattered throughout the penitentiary detected nothing suspicious. Some blamed the prison authorities, others the Judicial branch and even the Executive itself to be partly guilty of the escape, but no matter how many people were looking for those responsible, they did not find any and only went so far as to say that those who managed to enter and take those inmates were geniuses from the underworld. Never until that day had a jailbreak been so well planned and so masterfully organized that even left the local police spectacularly confused.

Since that fateful day, the authorities began a thorough investigation to capture the gang and even offered a reward of several thousand dollars for each inmate and the members of the crew who facilitated the escape. Every single organization out there made themselves available to help with the search; policemen, private guards, neighborhood committees… even the Interpol was notified in case the criminals fled the country. But there was a problem: nobody knew the real names or had seen the faces of the group of thugs who had organized the jailbreak. No one knew, except for the young detectives.

Meanwhile, at the Pardo Avenue apartment Ayesha and Schariar watched the news on TV. When Schariar found out that the criminals had fled the penitentiary, he got tense.

"Ayesha: I have a feeling that Smith and his crew are right now somewhere here in Lima."

Ayesha agreed with her friend.

"I'm afraid they'll come looking for us because of what we did to them last time. They may seek revenge."

"Don't worry. We are together. Besides, Smith is not vengeful criminal," Schariar replied.

"Hopefully it'll be as you say," Ayesha sighed. "What should we do now?"

"We'll think of something," Schariar replied as the phone started ringing. "Yes, hello? Who is this?"

"It's Lieutenant Richard," a manly voice replied. "Hello, young man, do you remember me?"

"Of course, how can I ever forget you? What's up?" Schariar said playing dumb.

"Are you kidding me? Don't you watch the news?"

"Oh, yes, yes, I heard something about a jailbreak… are you referring to that?"

"That's right," the lieutenant said, "And you will never guess who did it!"

"No idea whatsoever… let me guess: drug trafficker El Padrino."

"You are pulling my leg, right? It's the same crew we caught with your help… I called to ask for your help in this search, since you are the only ones who know their names… Of course, you will be given a very good reward and a badge of honor if we catch them."

"Let me think about it, lieutenant. The crew's boss is very smart."

"That's fine…" the lieutenant replied, "But maybe you'd like to give us their real names and physical characteristics so that we can start putting together their profiles…"

"I'm sorry, lieutenant, I really don't know their names. And what you're asking is more of a police matter. But if I change my mind, I'll let you know," the young detective lied in order to avoid getting hit with some type of revenge plot.

"Okay. I'll see you at the police station if you change your mind," the officer replied.

"Okay. Thank you for your time," Schariar said and he hung up the phone.

They began to ponder the situation of Smith and his gang, they were in doubt whether to accept or reject the lieutenant's offer. After all, it was a large sum of money and so much fame. After thinking about it for a while, they decided to accept the deal, but with the condition of not giving the thugs names or address to the police.

Ayesha reproached him for having lied to the police when saying that he did not know their names.

"Look Ayesha, I did it to protect us in case Smith captured us or we became revenge targets for one of the members of his crew. We will have points in favor when we remind him that we kept their identities before the authorities in complete anonymity. Remember that in the underworld if you're a snitch you end up paying a very high price for your betrayal," Schariar explained.

After he finished his conversation with Ayesha, Schariar picked up the phone and dialed the number of the police station. Once someone answered, he asked for Lieutenant Richard.

"Lieutenant: I called to tell you that we'll help you out. We'll come by tomorrow morning to get the proper authorization to start on the case," Schariar said.

"Of course, young man. I'm delighted to learn you'll work with us. I promise you'll have all of our support. I'll see you tomorrow."

"See you tomorrow, lieutenant."

It was the second time the young detectives would be involved in a police case, but this time they had the advantage of their first experience, the case of the thirteen gold coins.

Meanwhile in Magdalena, a district on the east side of Lima, Smith and his crew were having a great time talking and laughing and remembering how they fooled the guards during the jailbreak.

"Those guards were really stupid, and I know they will never catch us again, unless those young detectives look for us… As you know, they know our names and how we go about our business," Javier said.

"Don't worry," Smith replied, "Those kids won't bother us anymore. And if they did, I'm pretty sure they will not give our names to the police. Rest assured. Now, the plan: we'll hijack a Peruvian airline Boeing 707 that in four days, at 2:15 in the morning, will be flying to Madrid, Spain. That plane will carry important people. According to my plan, and involving certain key people already positioned at the highest levels of government and military, we could arrange for an amazing takeover of power and with that we would ensure nobody in this world can stop us. I only have to make sure that first we neutralize those meddling young people."

Part IV
Confidential Information

First thing next morning Schariar and Ayesha got ready to go to the police station, got into the car and they drove there together.

When they got there, they were able to quickly meet Lieutenant Richard to sit down and get up to date on everything the authorities could disclose so far.

"As you know, my dear friends, we don't have precise information regarding the jailbreak. What we do know, is that two people were able to get in the penitentiary pretending to be guards, they crossed all the blocks making a mockery of all the surveillance, took their comrades out of jail and left through a tunnel that leads to the main courtyard. From there we assume that they climbed the wall, unless someone else had helped them from outside."

"Lieutenant, you're saying that someone physically on the outside of the penitentiary helped them, but… don't they also have guards in the surrounding areas?" Schariar wanted to know.

"Of course, the entire perimeter is guarded. That's why we cannot understand how they manage to get away with outdoing every single guard," Lieutenant Richard replied. "I know it's a unique investigation, that's why we are asking for your specific help. Because you are the only ones who know more than us about that criminal organization."

Ayesha noticed that the lieutenant made a long pause. She asked, “What’s going on, lieutenant? You look disconcerted.”

The lieutenant looked at the girl, lit a cigarette and after finding a way to relax, he answered her question.

“Yes, I am, my friends; and it’s because I cannot understand how, having methods of study, experience and the necessary technology for the fight against crime here and in the world, nobody can win against that crew. However, you know everything.”

It was like he had said, “I am already old and there are things here that I still cannot understand: two groups in struggle, both move in the low and dark backgrounds of society; one of them, on the sidelines and supporting the law, and the other, against it.”

"Oh, my lieutenant! Someday you will find out how a systems student and a chemical engineering student got involved in this kind of business, it seems like a novel written by a Platonic idealist," Ayesha said.

"Lieutenant, you told me that there were two people who entered the prison disguised as guards, who gave you that information? I would like to visit the prison and find out what other intel can be obtained, is that okay?" Schariar said.

"Agreed," the lieutenant quickly answered. "And regarding the info: it was given to me by the guards at the door in addition to what was recorded by video camera 1 in the area of prisoner intake."

"Very well. What we need now is an authorization letter to get into the penitentiary and conduct our own investigation," Schariar replied.

"Perfect! And since I was expecting that answer from you; before you came, I prepared this signed document giving you the lead on this case and promising our complete support," the lieutenant replied.

"Well, with that taken care, we are ready to get going, lieutenant, we'll circle back with you as soon as we have fresh info."

"Thanks, young man, and good luck."

The meeting ended there, and the young detectives officially got started on the case.

But, before leaving, the young man wedged an electronic device under the lieutenant's desk --it allowed him to listen to the conversations at that office while wirelessly connected to his computer. The device's battery would last a little bit over two weeks.

The young man wedged an electronic device under the lieutenant's desk --it allowed him to listen to the conversations at that office while wirelessly connected to his computer. The device's battery would last two weeks.

As soon as the young detectives left, the lieutenant communicate with an unidentified person.

"XI, be careful, the young detectives will be looking for you. Don't let them close. Make her your prisoner," the lieutenant said.

"Thanks for the tip, lieutenant. We'll talk before our "special" day. Okay? Over and out."

Meanwhile, the young friends went to the prison to investigate and collect clues.

Upon arrival they observed a rather gloomy and unpleasant place, especially for a person like Ayesha, accustomed to a comfortable life thanks to the efforts of her father. Schariar, however, even though he also came from a "good" family, had already been in many poor and dreary places in the city.

The penitentiary was a large building surrounded by a solid wall five meters tall. There were guard towers on each corner, high-voltage lights and security alarms. When they arrived and showed their permission, they let them in, and offer all the help the young detectives needed. The investigation turned a bit tedious because Schariar would talk to each and every guard and employee. They visited the block that held immates who had committed crimes against personal property. They walked until they reached a spot where the path became narrower and darker. They could hardly see. A guard told them that this was the place for the immates who were serving life sentences. The place was a maze of passageways; and the guard pointed out that there was only one exit that could be reached after passing through a narrow tunnel that connected with the playground.

Schariar ordered the guard to show them that route. So, they walked for about ten or fifteen minutes in a darkness that seemed to go on forever. After, they entered through a tunnel where they had to crawl until they reached an opening and went out into the courtyard where the prisoners where allowed to be for some time during the day. Crossing that patio, they saw a fence, and from there, about thirty meters away, the dividing wall with the outside world.

Schariar was taking everything in. Once he was done looking around, he had a question for the guard.

"The security protocol during the day is the same one you have at night?"

The guard moved his head in affirmation.

As he watched the guards coming and going, Schariar would look at his wristwatch. Ayesha had no idea why he measured the time, but she could tell that he had gained more experience and intuition and even from time to time she was frightened by his sharpness. After a while they went to the exit area and started looking at the dirt that surrounded the prison until Schariar saw something strange.

"Ayesha come here!" he shouted, "Look at this, if you observe it well you'll realize that these are the marks left by dragging a person; and look at the grass on this place hidden here near the wall: it is more crushed, as if they had put weight on it; and it looks the same on the other side of the penitentiary. Ayesha, today's policemen disappoint me; or maybe someone within the government is involved in this jailbreak and they do not want it to be made known. Let's go home and I'll explain to you how they escaped. I already have all the info I need."

They got in the car and drove to the Pardo Avenue apartment. There, Schariar started to share what he was thinking.

"You'll remember, Ayesha, when we caught Smith and his crew," he said.

"Of course," she replied.

"And you'll remember that Smith fled the office of the prefect."

"Of course."

"Well, Smith and that partner were the two people who managed to get their five other fellow crewmembers, the prisoners. At the entrance door there were five guards in the night, two in the towers of the front and three at the door, making a round. I do not know why one of them and then the other reached the corner and turned to the side. But it was at that moment that the thugs caught them, immobilized them and put on their military uniform. They did the same with the other. Then, dressed as guards, it is easy to imagine how they entered the prison, they could've done it when the guards changed shifts. Then they looked for the master of the keys, gagged him and, after studying the map of the prison, they went to the block that held the inmates held for crimes against property, not without first having to circumvent some guards and acting violently against some others. After, they quickly went to cells 8, 9 and 10 of Block 6 and rescued their friends. They continued walking towards where the prisoners serving life sentences lived, they crossed the tunnel to the patio, quickly reached the fence, passing underneath, and from there on to the wall in less than three minutes, which is the time that takes the guards to turn and cross each other. Once they reached the wall, someone from outside must have helped them."

"But, Schariar, it's posible that it was only Smith that went in."

"I don't think so, Ayesha, because overtaking two trained guards before crossing the block is not easy, it must have been two people; and do not forget that Betty, Smith's girlfriend, is also free; or some new member gave them help. Once out of prison they would meet somewhere in the capital. As you can see, it's very clear, I do not know why the police are having so much trouble getting to the bottom of this jailbreak. What we have to figure out now is where they are and what are they planning."

"Oh my God, Schariar, every day you surprise me even more," Ayesha replied with admiration. "If I wasn't here with you I wouldn't believe that you were able to reveal details not even the police have uncovered."

"Come on, Ayesha, it's not that hard. I used my intuition. But right now, it's very important that nobody finds out what we already know. We'll let them know everything when the proper time comes. What does baffle me, Ayesha, is that one of the guards told me that the man disguised as a policeman who came to take his fellow inmates showed him a paper with a court order to take one of the prisoners. Although he realized that the man had already been prosecuted, the guard could not refuse because the document had the seal and signature of the judge on duty."

"Well, I think that means that that judge is on Smith's side," Ayesha replied.

"I thought exactly that myself, my friend, and I asked the guard. He assured me that it could not be so since there were also some writings that modified the order, but with so little difference in the wording that they did not care about it. And saying this, the guard continued saying: 'Besides, I think that there are people within the Government involved in this jailbreak.'"

"That's a problem, Shariar. It means that this time it would be very difficult for us to get close and catch Smith," Ayesha replied astounded.

“You are correct, my friend, that’s why I was about to tell you that I should do this by myself.”

“No. I won’t allow it! I’ll go with you wherever you go… even if we have to face death itself.”

Amazed by the response he received from her, Schariar thanked her for trusting him and, after a short time looking at her, he replied that he was going to go out alone, to walk and organize his ideas and that he would be back in a few minutes

Before ending their chat, they heard on their computer the conversation that came to them through the microphone that he placed in the lieutenant's office.

Schariar walked along the boardwalk looking out to the sea and thinking about everything that had happened to him in the last year; Smith and his gang, his car, the police, criminals and many other things. At some point he started shuddering without knowing for sure if it was out of fear or passion for the adventure.

He couldn't believe how his life had taken such a dizzying turn. Immersed in his thoughts, he remembered his friend Ayesha: with long blonde hair, light-colored eyes and slender frame, looking at him, advising him as always. He couldn't pinpoint exactly what was it, but something was happening inside him. Every time he was with her, he felt more calm and secure. With these thoughts in mind he started to walk the way back, always on the Miraflores boardwalk, toward his place.

Right at that moment they knocked on the door three times in the apartment on Pardo Avenue. Ayesha, thinking it was her friend, ran to open the door. When she saw that it was nobody, she closed it again, but before she was done, she noticed an envelope on the floor addressed to them. She closed the door and went to sit in the living room to open it and see what it said.

Dear Schariar:

Im writing to inform you that we are free to go for a rematch. You will remember the last time we met, right? Well, now we have an advantage: we know you and you do not know where we are. We will keep in communication.

Sincerely,

Smith Cross

You can imagine how upset Ayesha was after reading the letter, and even worst when she realized that only a few minutes ago one of Smith's friends had been on the other side of her door… What would have happened to her if one of the thugs had entered? She couldn't believe it. As she was thinking all those horrible thoughts someone knocked three times at the door and than the doorknob started to turn.

At that moment there were three slight touches to the door and after a few seconds the hand began to turn. You could imagine how she was feeling. She hid behind the bar that was located three meters from the door, grabbing a porcelain vase to throw it to the first one who entered. A few seconds of tension passed, and if it were not for the agility of Schariar he would have ended up in the hospital, because just as he opened the door and entered, the first thing he saw was a white thing that was going straight to his face. Thankfully, he managed to bend, and the vase crashed on the wall near the edge of the door. Upon reacting, the first thing Schariar saw was her friend hiding behind the furniture crying. He approached her and after lifting and holding her, Schariar asked her what had happened and why she threw the vase that almost sent him to intensive care.

As she sobbed and wiped away her tears, Ayesha told him what had happened since he went out for a walk. Once he knew what had happened, the young man leaned back on the couch and laughed. Ayesha did not understand. Anger overtook her, and she started to try punching Schariar as he managed to dodge her while laughing. Finally, Schariar came to his senses, and, trying to reassure her, he held her face with both hands and explained why he laughed, he said it was because now it was Smith who wrote to them and not them to him, as they used to do. After calming down, each went to their room to rest.

The next day, after breakfast, Schariar asked Ayesha if any other letter had been left under that door.

She replied she had not seen anything.

"Okay. In that case, we'll leave the apartment through the emergency exit and we'll sit and wait at some place from where we can see our apartment without being seen until we find our suspects."

"And what if they don't come back, Schariar?" she replied.

"That's not possible," Schariar replied, "they'll come back. I know they will come back."

Part V
Looking for Clues

That was a frustrating day for Schariar as he waited for a suspect and looked, without results, for a clue that would lead him to Smith and his crew.

"Let's go home Schariar. It's ten at night and we need to rest. Tomorrow is going to be a long day, but I'm sure we'll do much better," Ayesha said.

"You're right," Schariar replied, "Besides, I'm tired and hungry. I have not even had a slice of bread all day. Let's go. This time I'm going to side with you."

But as they were returning along Pardo Avenue to the apartment, Schariar was not very happy with the idea of resting and leaving the way clear to Smith. Ayesha, who knew her friend very well, observed in him a great concern while Schariar tried not to let her see it.

When they got home, they made sandwiches and coffee. After eating, they went to sleep.

This would be a good time to point out that Ayesha was independent from her parents. She did it after explaining to them in every possible way that she would be fine, and introducing her friend Schariar to them, who made sure she had her own room in his apartment. He was a true gentleman always, even though she would have loved to sleep in the same room with him. She had special feelings for him, even though she couldn't put in words why was she attracted to Schariar.

When Ayesha got up and went to the kitchen to prepare breakfast before leaving, she realized that her friend was not in his room. Apparently Schariar had left very early, and when she looked at the alarm clock and noticed that it was two o'clock in the morning, Ayesha worried for a moment; she did not know why he would've left at dawn; but then she calmed down thinking that lately he had changed a lot and he liked to investigate at night more than during the day.

She went to the window and looked at the damp and misty street. Almost in a whisper he murmured, "I hope he took his coat."

Suddenly, she was surprised to see Schariar's black car parked in the same place where they left it the night before, she remained pensive and astonished, she did not understand why this time he acted so differently.

“It’s okay,” she said to herself, “I’m sure he’ll be back soon, and I have to finish this college report if I ever want to get to my last semester.”

At around six in the afternoon the door opened and Schariar came in. Ayesha had fallen asleep at her desk while doing her report. She woke up and when she saw the obvious signs of fatigue on his friend’s face and his dirty clothes she worried about him a lot. She helped him to go to his room and later brought him something to eat. He asked her to leave him alone and not to worry. He said that he was not hungry and that he wanted to organize his ideas as well as the clues he found while he was out. Shortly after Ayesha left the room, Schariar fell into a deep state of sleep.

Half an hour later, Ayesha came back to Schariar's room to put a blanket over him since she worried he would catch a cold; but while she did this, Ayesha kissed him on the forehead.

Schariar woke up at around ten at night and walked to the living room where he put the TV on to watch the news. He couldn't understand why Smith was still in Perú and had not yet left and go to some other country. As he meditated, he heard on the news that a delegation of diplomats and military personnel from the country were going to travel to Brussels for an international meeting on world peace. The group would depart in two days but for security reasons the government was not sharing details of the trip, such as time or airline or where they would travel.

As he heard the news, Schariar thought of the only other option that had not crossed his mind until then.

“Someone is getting kidnapped! I’m an idiot for not figuring it out earlier! Now I understand the newspaper, the uniforms, the judge’s order, the radio broadcast, and that guard that told me that people at the government level were involved in the jailbreak!” Schariar talked to himself while pacing around the room. “And what about the Army? They must be part of all of this! I’ll have to go out again tonight.”

When Schariar heard the news, he exclaimed, "It's a kidnapping! I should've figure it out before. Now I understand."

In that moment the phone rang. When he answered, he heard Lieutenant Richard's voice asking him if he knew anything about the gang. Schariar replied that not yet, and that he had not yet found any leads regarding them.

"Fine. I just received information that they might have fled crossing the north border this morning. I guess we don't have to worry about it any longer because the case is in the hands of Interpol," the lieutenant replied.

Upon hearing that statement Schariar could not help but smile as he told the lieutenant that if he was sure of it, that the group was no longer in the country, then he could rest easy. Then he said goodbye politely.

As he hung up the phone, Schariar smiled again as he said to himself, "What they don't know is that I know their plan."

But Schariar did not suspect that that conversation was also a trick for him to fall into the trap.

"If I told the lieutenant that Smith and his crew are here in Lima, and near the airport, it would ruin everything. Smith must not get away with it! I've almost formulated a plan and it will work."

In that moment Ayesha came in and when she saw him with a strange expression she became extremely concerned.

"Even after sleeping you look weird! I recommend you go to the doctor and see what's wrong with you," she said to Schariar.

"You're wrong, Ayesha! I'm okay. The problem is that I have several leads but can't find the truth yet. I'll go out again tonight," he replied.

“I can go with you,” she offered.

“That’s not necessary, my friend. I don’t want to put you in risk,” he replied.

“But I’ll be concerned. I won’t be able to sleep knowing that something bad can happen to you,” she complained.

“No! This is an important night in the investigation. You can come with me tomorrow.”

Ayesha didn’t take his response well but, as you’ll find out later, he was right.

“But, Schariar, this time you are doing everything by yourself. You don’t care for my observations any more. If that’s the case, I better leave, and we’ll go our separate ways,” Ayesha replied in anger.

Schariar did not know what to say, he understood very well that what he was going to do was dangerous, but he did not want Ayesha to leave either, so he tried to persuade her. But she, returning to her old personality, from before meeting him, put together all her things in a suitcase and left for her parents' house, although deep down she did not want to do that.

She had no way of knowing that the minute she stepped on the street and walked to the corner to hail a taxi there will be three people there, waiting to kidnap her.

They blindfolded her and, tying her hands and feet, they placed her in a red Toyota Celica and headed for some place in Callao.

Meanwhile Schariar ran to the street to intercept her and tell her how much he loved her and needed to have her with him; but when he turned the corner he saw three people holding Ayesha and forcing her into a car. He ran to stop them, but it was too late; the car was already running and he, even if he was close to his car, could not have reached them even with the powerful turbines of his car.

After a while, he returned home pensive and meditative about what happened. He sat on the couch and turned on the television, but he could not concentrate on the images, he blamed himself for the danger that Ayesha was in at that moment. Without realizing it, he remembered Smith and the pending plan, so Schariar put on the clothes he had and took his motorcycle to the agreed place.

Part VI
A Secret Encounter

It was about ten o'clock at night and Schariar was lurking around the bridge that crosses the Rímac river, also known as the "talking river" in the language of the ancient inhabitants of the Lima valley, the main river that crosses the city of Lima and flows into the sea through the Callao area, near the main seaport of the country, close to Faucett Avenue, which is the main avenue that goes from south to north and arrives at the first airport in the country. Two people talked on the same bridge; one of them wore a military uniform; the other was white, tall and in civilian attire. After their short chat, they took a car that took them to the airport. The soldier introduced him to several people who worked at the airline. After five minutes they said goodbye and the man in civilian clothes got into an almost new red Toyota Celica with license plate Q6-3646 and drove to 646 Los Cedros Street in Vipol.

Schariar followed them from the bridge to the airport to the house. When they arrived at Los Cedros, he hid behind some bushes from where he could see the side window and hear their conversation.

"Hey, boss, we just kidnapped the girlfriend of that young detective that meddled so much into our business last time," Javier Lamp said as he greeted Smith.

"That's great," Smith replied, "Go ahead and bring her to me so we can have a little talk."

You can imagine how Schariar was feeling as he saw Ayesha in the hands of his worst enemy. He wanted so badly to go in and confront Smith! But he knew that could be dangerous and would place Ayesha in harms way. So, he kept all his strength and kept spying on them.

"So, you've been spying on us?"

"That's right. I'm not afraid of you," Ayesha replied

"Yes, I see that, I like it when my enemy is brave, but you do not know what you are exposing yourself to. Of course, because you are the friend of my most admired enemy, you have gained my respect, and now you'll serve as bait so that he'll be forced to come to me,"

Smith said without imagining that he was being listened to by the young detective.

Smith ordered that Ayesha be locked up and not be harmed; that order was especially directed at Pedro, who everybody knew had a lustful mind. He also told Carlos, Edward and Javier Lamp to look around the house to make sure no one had followed them after they kidnapped her. They had no idea that the young man was already on his way to the airport to find out about that airline.

As soon as he arrived, Schariar approached the window and, pretending to be a lost passenger, asked for a military man in a thousand possible ways, until the receptionist realized who was the person he was talking about and informed him that he was one of the people responsible for the entry of the passengers to the airport, Navy Captain Óscar Avilés. When Schariar asked her something else, she replied that it was a private matter and that there was nothing else she could tell him. So, Schariar said goodbye to the young lady while leaving a tiny microphone stuck under the counter.

That night Schariar was restless and slept very little, he was concerned for Ayesha's fate and felt guilty because he decided to share with her that she would be going out at nighttime.

He woke up early the next morning, at around four in the morning, and without even thinking about it, he got dressed and went out looking for an open bar. Since it was Saturday, he had no problem finding one. He drank several beers, and at dawn, around 6:30 in the morning he went back to his apartment.

When Schariar got to his place, he noticed the door was completely opened, and as he entered and saw sofas overturned and curtains torn down, he realized in horror that he was the victim of some robbery. Maybe it was luck or a premonition, but apparently going out that night saved him from being present when some thugs committed a crime in his apartment.

With fear in his eyes, he quickly entered his room and, with a shudder, observed that everything was in complete disarray. Happily, it seemed that they did not find what they were looking for and Schariar gave thanks for leaving that night earlier than usual. While going through the damage, he found a letter in the handwriting of his friend Ayesha. He got emotional as he opened it.

My dearest friend and beloved Schariar:

I'm okay. Don't worry for me. Smith will call you when he feels it's appropriate. Do not do anything because it'll put me in danger. What happened to you tonight is a warning, but he says that the next time it may cost you your life.

Good-bye,

Ayesha

Schariar did not know what to do, he understood that if Smith learned of his plan or if he continued to do it, he would be in danger; but what worried him the most was his friend. While thinking and reflecting about this, he started to pace. At some point, a light behind him hit the paper he was still holding and underneath the handwriting he saw some signs. Schariar drew what he saw in another paper, and it resulted in a message.

ナΣ. 刀ᆕ⋇Σ ㄨ୨刀 •••⩨• ㄨ卞ㄨ

Once he realized what was going on, he exclaimed, "You are a genious, Ayesha."

And even thought he did not remember right away all the details about their secret code language, little by little it came back to him until he decoded the symbols into letters:

Av. Perú SMP 381 / S O S

Schariar had resolved the puzzle and apparently Smith did not notice when she posted the message. As he read the address Schariar also realized that Smith and his crew had moved to some other place.

"If it were not for that visit we made to the museum and the creation of our own secret language, without knowing that very soon we would use it, I would not know what to do right now. Ayesha: that's why I love you more every day and if it were possible I would give my life for you. As the saying states: you are worth a Peru," Schariar said to his missing friend.

And returning to the problem, what to do in the future without Smith suspecting, he thought of two options: One was to act violently, break into their hiding place and take them by surprise; and the second path was to meet with the commander general of the Armed Forces or even with the Peruvian president and tell them everything.

But he had a bad feeling, currently the Armed Forces were going through a strong political crisis and Captain Óscar Avilés had great influence over a certain group of soldiers and, if they were united with Smith and perpetrated the kidnapping, it was easy to imagine a coup d'etat, since in those moments the military high command would be kidnapped and therefore the Peruvian president would not even find out until it was too late.

He spent the morning playing scenarios in his mind. He needed to act cautiously but strongly. If he was correct about what was going on, his decisions would affect the entire country.

It was 2:30 in the afternoon when Schariar headed to the police station to meet Lieutenant Richard. As he left his apartment and drove through the streets of Lima he made sure nobody was following him.

Schariar found the lieutenant in his office. Once they were alone, the young detective informed the officer that everything he was about to say was highly confidential.

"Of course, Schariar, I'm listening," Lieutenant Richard said, "Although I really don't know what else is there to discuss since Smith and his crew are already out of the country."

"Don't make me laugh, lieutenant, that gang is still here, and closer than you can imagine. What I'm about to say cannot leave this room."

"Alright. I promise. Talk already. You're making me curious," Lieutenant Richard replied.

"Okay. First of all, my colleague has been kidnapped by them. So, everything I'm about to do is for her, to get her out. Second, I'm almost sure they are planning a coup d'etat and some sort of kidnapping. I need to talk with the president."

"The Peruvian president? Come on, Schariar, what you ask is almost impossible. Tell you what: if you give me that address you have, we'll go and apprehend them right away."

Schariar felt he needed to lie to protect the intel he gathered.

"I can't give you the address. They've moved, and I don't know where to. But there's something else: I'm looking for background info on Navy Captain Óscar Avilés," he said.

"That's confidential information, Schariar."

Schariar felt frustrated by the lieutenant's objections.

"I think it was a mistake on my part coming here to seek your help, lieutenant. You are only one more person that can't help. I'll go ahead and look for a way to talk to the president himself," Schariar replied. As he said good-bye and prepared to leave the office he took the old microphone and left a new one underneath the lieutenant's desk.

As he walked the streets of downtown Lima, Schariar realized that the device that was connected to the microphone at the lieutenants' office started to blink its red light. He knew what that meant. He intercepted the communication to listen in.

"Sergeant Sergio, I inform you that the young detective suspects our coup against the government and our relationship with Smith. You need to get your people to get to him and make him disappear, understood?

"Of course, my lieutenant, I assure you it'll be done no later than tonight."

Schariar finally had the evidence he needed to deliver the final blow. He had the names of almost all the military involved in the coup, almost everyone who had searched at the beginning to catch Smith was part of the plot.

The lieutenant himself, who was his man of confidence at the beginning, was now his enemy. He sat for a while on the side of a church in downtown Lima and reflected for a while about what he should do given those circumstances.

And than he made up his mind and chose a path: the only one he could've taken given what he knew, the riskiest choice he had been thinking about…

Part VII
The Interview

That night at about one o'clock in the morning the Plaza de Armas of Lima was like any night: quiet, peaceful and regal. Nothing foreshadowed that something would happen. However, the cord of the telephone line that communicated with the Presidential Palace shook in an unusual way, and, without the guards noticing, a man dressed in black who was hanging from the cable and moving down with the help of a spinning wheel, subreticiously finished sliding the telephone cord, reached the roof of the palace, where he hid for a moment, then jumped to hit the guards knocking them against a door and rendering immediately unconscious.

The dark figure ran to the door and as he was going to open it, someone did it from the other side, which forced him to hide again.

As two guards came out for their shift and to relieve their mates, the man in black took the opportunity to enter and then walked down a long corridor, lit with a few spotlights of dim light; then he went down the stairs to the first floor and tried to approach the bedrooms, but not before having to hide and wait for the guards to pass about ten times. He arrived first at the kitchen, then at another room and thinking that this was the one he was looking for, he manipulated it with special wires until it opened.

Upon entering and illuminating it with his flashlight he realized that it was a storage room. As he shined the flashlight around, a black cat jumped on top of him and fled quickly causing the man to scream in silence.

He continued on his search, and after about ten minutes he passed through the entrance hall of the Palace and finally arrived at the bedrooms; the first was of the president's children and the second was of the president.

He couldn't believe it. He had passed all the security barriers of the Presidential Palace without even being seen.

"Now I'm a real ninja. It's like I'm invisible to everybody," the man snickered to himself while he hid from two guards that went right by him and continued walking until they got lost in the shadows.

He stood up from his hiding place and, approaching the bedroom door, manipulated it with his set of secret keys. A couple of "clicks" sounded and the lock was free.

With excitement and nervousness he pushed the door gently and entered the room, closing the door very slowly. He turned on the light and when he looked in front of himself, he could not help but to tremble with emotion, the Peruvian president look back at him. He was there by himself. The man thought to himself that he had the president at his mercy. He could kill him or do anything to him, and nobody would know it was him since he planned to leave the same way he came in.

But he was not a criminal and he didn't come into the president's bedroom with bad intentions. On the contrary, he was there to inform the president about what was being planned behind his back.

He approached slowly and upon reaching the left side of his bed he gently woke him up. As he opened his eyes, the president saw the man dressed in black and started shouting, calling for his bodyguards. Annoyed, Schariar took off his hood and quickly introduced himself as a servant of the nation that was there to tell him everything he knew. Realizing that he was not in danger and that, quite the opposite, he was going to find out about things he did not even imagine, the president calmed down; so that when his personal guards approached the door and asked what was going on, he calmed them down saying it was just a dream and not to worry.

Once the president was ready to listen, the young detective told him everything he knew and presented his plan to stop the kidnapping and the coup d'état.

"There's a group of people planning a coup d'état. And if you allow me, I'll tell you everything," Schariar explained.

The president was stunned for a moment; he did not know if it was a joke or if they really wanted to kill him. After a moment he asked, "How did you manage to enter the Palace?"

"It was easy. Your security team could take lessons from me."

"Okay… Suppose I believe you… I need to know: how did you get your intel?"

Schariar interrupted the president. "If you wish to continue this conversation, we should go to a more private place, somewhere like your office, so that no one listens to all of this."

Before getting up, the president told Schariar that he was not comfortable believing someone he didn't know but that, somehow, he seemed trustworthy.

After the president dressed up, the two men left the room and walked down the hallway to the president's office. When the guards saw the president accompanied by the young man heading to that place they could not help but to be surprised, asking each other where he had come from. But nothing could be done since the president himself was treating him as he knew him.

Once inside the presidential office, and with the door closed, Schariar told him everything from the beginning, even showing him evidence of the conversations, he had intercepted on several occasions with his microphone hidden in the desk of the lieutenant, the police, and in the airport, as you, our readers, already know, so I won't repeat it here.

Surprised by the story, the president congratulated the young man for his audacity, in addition to thanking him for the news of the revolt being planned by a military group. Immediately he called the commander general of the Armed Forces and the head of the intelligence services, and once they knew everything, and at about 3:30 a.m., they prepared a contingency plan called "master plan."

Part VIII
Master Plan Vs. Smith

On Monday (the next morning) in the office of military recruitment in Callao everything was running as any other day. The boys, all young people between 17 and 18 years of age, waited their turn for the medical examination and to find out which Navy battalion they would enter. After a long time of waiting, the reading of the list began, all of them lined up in an orderly fashion and waited for the judgement of the person in charge of the office.

"Let's see young men," the person in charge said. "Numbers 1 to 15 will go to the 20th batallion, from 16 through 35 will go to the 21st batallion…" and he kept reading until he reached the end of the list. "Numbers 145 through 170 are assigned to the 32nd batallion."

A naval officer upon hearing his battalion number was surprised and went immediately to the manager's office and told him the following:

"Lieutenant Roberto! Who gave that order that twenty-five young recruits enter our battalion? Or do you not remember that we are preparing them for another mission that will take place today at noon?"

"Captain," the lieutenant answered, "that order comes from higher ranks and there's nothing we can do. But if you feel we should not add these young men to your batallion, then feel free to change the list or to tell them it was a clerical error."

At that moment, the door opened, and the commander general of the Navy in Callao came in. After exchanging greetings, he asked while staring at the captain:

"Is there a problem with the list of new recruits?"

"There's not, commander," the captain and lieutenant replied with some nervousness.

After that brief exchange the commander general said goodbye and left.

"This does not feel right… I think they're suspicious," the captain said.

"I don't think so. You're just nervous," the lieutenant replied. "If they were suspicious, they would be hauling us out right now. And they haven't. It's just a coincidence. Calm down."

"And I think you are mistaken," the captain insisted. "But I'll try to resolve the situation with the new recruits some how. Anyway, don't forget to be at the place we agreed at four o'clock."

Meanwhile, at the airport, things were getting quite busy, the plane that would transport all of the nation's congress-people to the meeting in Brussels was ready. It was two o'clock in the afternoon when the representatives began to arrive. Between the military and the congressmen there were a total of thirty-five people. They identified themselves at the airline counter and then boarded the plane normally, but under strict surveillance.

Once the last representative had passed and the plane door closed, seven people dressed as flight crew removed their coats and with machine guns in their hands they made all the people there get flat on the floor. At that time fifty soldiers belonging to the 32nd batallion, of the sixty-five who cared for and guarded the airport, ordered all the entry and exit doors closed, disconnecting all the alarms and communication radios. Nobody realized that five minutes later a person communicated with the Peruvian president giving him all the information of the facts and congratulating him because everything was going as planned. The hijackers were inside the plane with the delegates.

Meanwhile, in downtown Lima, an aggressive military intervention was underway with shootings, grenades and even tanks taking on the streets. Two of the soldiers who guarded the Presidential Palace were killed because of their own mistakes. Others, unable to keep the soldiers in charge of executing the military coup from taking over had no choice but to surrender.

At that moment the man in charge of the entire rebel forces communicated by radio with Smith, who was inside the hijacked plane, informing him that they had achieved their objectives and that all that was left to do was to enter the Palace and remove the president. At that moment cheers and applause from the insurgent soldiers were heard when their leader, and next Peruvian president, entered the

Palace. But great was their surprise when they found the premises completely empty and a note for him.

Navy Captain Óscar Avilés:

I congratulate you for your ingenious performance, but we were already informed and now you have fallen into our trap.

President of the Republic

News Now - Associated Press

The television channels transmitted the results of the failed military coup.

"We've been informed by our correspondents in Lima of the events that are happening right now; a failed coup d'état and apparently the hijacking of an airplane with military and political delegates. The person responsible for these events is the peruvian Navy Captain, Óscar Avilés, who was apparently discovered by a young detective whose name has not been revealed as it is a state secret. This young man was the architect of a master plan that freed this South American country from of a possible military coup.

Surrounded by the military forces and facing dire circumstances at this hour, because of the failed plan, the Navy captain is holding out, together with several of his subordinates and high-power weapons, and is asking for assurances that he and his people will be able to leave alive and board a helicopter they are requesting in order to leave the country safe and sound.

At this time, we apologize for the interruptions of the signal, but this is caused by several MIG16 airplanes flying around downtown Lima and tanks of the Army's first

Infantry division guarding the entire city to avoid any response from the coup. Apparently, they have everything under control and, according to an anonymous military source, this will be resolved no later than tonight. The main international airport of the country, located in the port of Callao, is also being taken over by the military and they inform us that there have been several casualties, although they tell us that the situation is already under control.

We will keep you informed as more news unfold. Have safe afternoon.

Associated Press".

The television channels returned to their regular daytime programs to keep the audience entertained while soldiers and officers performed their duties. Even so, there was an atmosphere of great tension in the capital city. People stopped working, and many businesses, to avoid looting or similar problems, closed until everything went back to normal. An hour went by since the last broadcast of the Associated Press when they unexpectedly returned on television to report...

News Now - Associated Press

"We are connecting with our correspondents in the city of Lima (Perú) who are informing us about a last-minute event.

We are told that an Army squadron specially trained for terrorism cases has taken control of the hijacked plane, it is known that there have been three casualties of the rebels and two soldiers are in critical condition —they have been transferred to the Naval Hospital to provide them with medical care.

They also inform us that three of the rebels have managed to escape without a trace. Police are searching for those fugitives by land and sea. All flights out of Lima's international airport have been suspended until further notice. The airport's main entrance doors are heavily guarded, and it is recommended that people and vehicles avoid taking the main streets and avenues that lead to this airport.

Also, two soldiers from the rebel side have died, murdered by their own group while trying to surrender before the Army took control of the airport."

There was an interruption of about thirty seconds while the journalists paused to talk about a new development. After that, they started reporting again.

"We are now informed that authorities have taken complete control of this airport. And right now, they are moving all the rebels to the Army's general headquarters in Callao; for their trial and sentencing. In addition, it is highly recommended not to drive or go boating in the area south of Lima since the search for the three fugitives is still going on.

Thank you very much and we will continue reporting as soon as we receive more news. Thank you and have a good night. Asssociated Press. Informing the world."

While newscasters reported on the unfolding events, Schariar was knocking down the door and forcibly entering Smith's secret house, located on Perú Avenue in the district of San Martín de Porres in Lima, along with three men from the Criminal Investigations Police. They did not face much resistance because they found Smith's girlfriend alone taking care of the young detective's friend as a hostage. Schariar, as always with his big heart after his anger had disappeared, and considering that his friend had not suffered damage, tried to persuade the three officers who accompanied him to let the girl out and that he did not have nothing to see in all that. Although deep down he knew the truth, for some inexplicable reason, the young detective felt a respect for Smith and he knew the criminal felt the same for him.

Conclusion

That day the young detectives left the scene shortly after answering some questions to the authorities. Once they got home, they communicated through social media with the Peruvian president. They wanted to find out if everything went well and if he was back at the Presidential Palace.

They were informed that Captain Óscar Avilés and the rebels, who were holding out inside the president's residence, started to fall apart the minute they found out their coup had failed. Eight of them surrendered and would be sent to court the next day. Any of them could get up to 25-years in jail, depending of their involvement. However, Captain Avilés and one of his aides couldn't take their failure or the thought of going to jail, and they took their lives with a shot to the head.

Three members of Smith's crew died during the battle of the airport. Carlos Chuquihuanca came out of it fine but killed himself cutting his throat with a knife while being taken into custody. He couldn't live with the fact that his boss abandoned him or that he was now heading to jail.

After all that mess, the one who did best was the young detective Schariar for having been the one who provided the information of the rebellion and prepared the counterattack.

When the young man rescued Ayesha and released Betty, as if he had not seen her, in her desperate escape she took some of Smith's money leaving a balance of $80,000 in a bag. The young man, as a good detective, took it as his reward in addition to receiving honors from the Peruvian president plus the reward of $100,000 dollars. The young man thanked him for the recognition, but he did not accept any position within the government, simply because he liked to be free and he did not like to be attached to a certain system of life. In addition, he knew that sooner or later he would confront Smith again, and it would be better if he were on his own than representing some police institution, he liked to go unnoticed, living in wealthy, gloomy, dark, and miserable neighborhoods. He felt that the more hidden he remained in society, the better he would live his life and the more prepared he would be to remain at the same level as his enemy.

The president accepted the young man's response willingly, and Schariar jokingly replied that with all the cases he was working he was earning a great amount of money that was becoming savings for his retirement. After that they said good-bye all the while loudly laughing.

And with this we finish, dear readers, with the story of the young detectives until their next adventure. And we will go on to report what happened with Smith, his bodyguard and his girlfriend Betty.

Epilogue

Around midnight, a little bit south of the Jorge Chávez International Airport in Callao, Betty was meeting with Smith Cross, Javier Lamp, and Gregory Bunge. After hugging for a long time, they went to a deserted beach, with no lights around and where they could not be seen. It was Ventanilla, a seashore city where during the day a few bathers could be seen since they lived in the city of the same name in poorly constructed houses of adobe that hardly have electricity or drinking water, aside from the community tap. A city founded by invaders, without any planning of its streets; and whose residents organizing independently forged with their shovels and picks their own roads and streets.

A perfect place to hide near their shore a boat that seemed like nothing special but whose powerful engines gave the ship the appearance of levitating above the sea while leaving a trail of white foam as it passed. The four crew members: Smith, Betty, Javier and Gregory boarded the ship and while the engines started to push the ship away from the coast they symbolically said goodbye to the country in which they had been staying for more than half a year, and where they didn't do as good as they envisioned due to the intrusion of some young detectives.

In the distance you could hear some light aircraft and helicopters from the Army scouring the coast in search of the fugitives.

Smith Cross smiled as he stood at the stern, watching as the shore started to dissapear, and he said goodbye. Betty took a handkerchief that hung from her shoulder, a pink handkerchief that had belonged to Ayesha and that she gave to Betty in a gesture of gratitude for having taken care of her. She waved it in the wind as if saying goodbye and threw a rose into the sea as her final farewell.

Smith, now the captain of the ship, ordered to keep steering away from the shore until the ship were out of the sight of the coastguard and from there on to Panama. His destination was Italy, Europe. To meet Mario Cassimiro who was waiting for them...

Smith Cross smiled as he stood at the stern, watching as the shore started to disappear.

Table of Contents

www.ingramcontent.com/pod-product-compliance
Lightning Source LLC
LaVergne TN
LVHW091005080826
845145LV00003B/1138

* 9 7 8 1 6 3 0 6 5 1 0 6 0 *